Also by C. D. ROSE

The Biographical Dictionary of Literary Failure
  (Melville House)

'Arkady Who Couldn't See and Artem Who
  Couldn't Hear' (Galley Beggar)

THE
NEVA STAR

C. D. ROSE

DAUNT BOOKS

First published in 2015 by
Daunt Books
83 Marylebone High Street
London W1U 4QW

1

Copyright © C. D. Rose 2015

A CIP catalogue record for this title is
available from the British Library.

ISBN 978 1 907970 81 8

Typeset by Antony Gray
Printed and bound by TJ International

www.dauntbookspublishing.co.uk

THE NEVA STAR

THERE IS A SHIP moored in the port of Naples that has been there for three years. In all this time, it has moved no more than a few inches, backwards and forwards, from side to side. This is not an entirely unusual situation as there are many ships in many ports around the world which have found themselves abandoned by bankrupted owners, impounded by national authorities, deserted by soon-to-be ex-magnates, orphaned by unpaid bills. In Genoa there is a ship that has been there for five years, and in Venice one for seven. An old ship moored in the port of Naples for three years is not an entirely unusual situation. All over the seafaring world there are ships that are flying the flag of the Bolivian and Mongolian merchant navies.

The *Neva Star* is a large dry cargo and tanker ship, designed for sea and river use with a reinforced hull so it can break ice from Archangels to Murmansk. It is registered in Odessa and is as rusty as a nail. It is 115 metres long and has three thin decks. It is painted orange and white. The bottom part of the ship is orange, the upper part white. White and rust, orange and rust. The ship was built in Romania 35 years ago and has since travelled over twenty thousand miles, sailing from Valletta to Leith to Rotterdam, from unlikely capital to unlikely capital, back to Odessa where it began and, now, to Naples.

*

Of the crew of seventy, sixty-seven have disappeared. There are now only three sailors on board. The three sailors have been there for three years. Three years plus the three months they spent arriving in Naples from Odessa. Nobody knows what happened to the captain.

Sergei, the first mate, passes much of his time thinking of his wife Masha. He has lived with Masha since St Petersburg was called Leningrad. Once, many years ago, Masha had the chance to leave Russia and go to Israel. She packed her small black leather bag with everything she had and got on the tram and sat there circling the canals of the Fontanka for hours. Late that evening, she arrived back home. Sergei opened the door of their flat to find her standing on the doorstep crying. He had

5

absolutely no idea why she had arrived home late, crying. This is one of the things he remembers as he passes away the many days lying on the small bunk in the same cabin he has slept in for more than three years. He still doesn't know why Masha arrived home late that evening, her cheeks wet with secrets.

Sergei, another of the sailors, occasionally finds himself thinking about the time when returning from a voyage to Cuba he and his old friend the first mate Sergei took the trip from Odessa up to St Petersburg to visit Sergei's hometown. He stayed for a week with Sergei and Sergei's wife Masha in their small flat on the twelfth floor of an apartment block on Ploshad' Musžestva. Their flat was as small as a ship's cabin, he remembers, although the view from the window was always the same. Now, out of the small porthole in his cabin on the *Neva Star*, the view is always the same.

Sergei hasn't seen his wife for five years. They met at a party when they were eighteen and married soon after. Three months later, Tatiana disappeared. Sergei wasn't worried. He heard she had gone to Moscow and moved in with a wealthy importer-exporter, and decided it was best to leave it there. Still, he sometimes misses her even though he now thinks he never really loved her. He thinks about Sergei's wife Masha, and the time when he stayed in their tiny apartment and the time when he kissed her once, very quietly and very quickly, while she was cooking potato soup in the kitchen. He wonders what the Italian girls are like. Before he disappeared, one of the other sailors – a

Romanian called Sorin – told Sergei about a friend of his who'd been stuck in Porto Marghera. He'd jumped ship and married the first girl he'd met, a Venetian. Sergei remembers reading somewhere that Venetian women are supposed to have webbed feet.

The third sailor is called Sergei. Sergei has often been tempted to chuck it all in and go onshore. If he got caught onshore, he'd risk getting sent back to Ukraine immediately and not be eligible for any pay for all the time he has spent on board the *Neva Star*, should it ever get out of Naples. This is why all three sailors stay on board. If they left, they would be summarily repatriated and forfeit any right to monies accruing. Sergei has heard that there are other Ukrainians in the city, though, and is sure that if he could find them he could set himself up here in Italy. Even though the others don't know it, Sergei has found eight hundred American dollars in a small bundle that smells of dried sweat in a worn brown envelope under the bunk in the captain's cabin.

There are three sailors left on board. They are all called Sergei. There is enough canned food on board to last them, they have calculated, for up to five years. They've been there for three years. They have enough canned food to last them another two.

Sergei, solid, dependable, practical and realistic, thinks it's better than the time he got stuck in Antwerp for three months. Even though he's been here for three years now and has never set foot on the land that is but a few metres away, he already knows that he likes Naples more than he liked Antwerp.

Here, the sky seems closer, heavier, bluer and thicker, especially when he thinks of the pale Baltic sky, distant, thin and airy. He sometimes wonders why a boat registered in Odessa should be called the *Neva Star* and, despite his solid, realistic practicality, can think of no other reason than some vague intention to make him feel even more homesick.

They've been there for three Augusts, when the bright heat is enough to split paving stones. It creeps on board like an animal and rubs around them, sticking to them like fur coats they can't take off. They've been there for three New Years, watching the fireworks over the city and listening to the other ships sound their horns at midnight, then celebrating their own muted vigil a week later, still obeying the Russian calendar, with one of the few bottles of *sovetskoe champanskae* that they have carefully stored away for New Year, Easter and three birthdays every year. They have already drunk all the vodka that was on board.

Sergei dreams all the time and not only when sleeping. He dreams of the sun sliding down the steps in Odessa, of his family and the house where he grew up. He dreams of being trapped on board the *Neva Star* for three years, of being on board this very ship, a dream which is inseparable from reality and this dream worries him. It worries him mostly because

11

in this dream there are only two of them, not three. He wonders what has happened to Sergei in his dream, but there's no answer. He has a bad dream where Tatiana's new husband comes looking for him armed with divorce papers which turn into a gun which turns into a dead fish. He dreams of Masha's trapped eyes and women with webbed feet. Waking, he remembers his dreams, then remembers the story: the travellers on the road to Emmaus. Wasn't it supposed to be two travellers who imagine a third? *Who is the third who walks always beside you?* Wasn't that the line? He wonders why he's dreaming the opposite.

When they go out on deck and look at the city beyond the docks, they see rows of white cement buildings and a wide road where cars speed past at all hours of the day and night. At night the road is dimly illuminated with fuzzy light, and they can see a few people loitering in the blocked yellow spaces under the shadows of the tall buildings.

Sometimes they are incessantly together, eating, sleeping, breathing and shitting in rhythm, all but holding hands for weeks at a time in a near hysterical attempt to ward off the vacuum of being alone. They have played more games of chess with each other than they can remember. Sergei always wins.

At other times they have spent months hardly talking to each other, going about their business (such business as they have) alone, spending time lying eyes open on their bunks, looking up, reading slowly so as not to finish the few books they have, not consciously avoiding each other but speaking little so as not to exhaust topics of conversation, moving slowly as if trying to conserve time, as if trying not to breathe too much for fear they'll use up all the air they have left.

Sergei has taken to disappearing when he thinks the others won't notice him gone. At night, usually, though sometimes during the day when it's quiet, he stretches a plank across the water and walks onto land. The solidity of the stone quay under his feet throws him off balance and makes him feel sick. He steals into the city, crossing the road with its deadly roaring traffic and scuttling up through the alleys that permeate the tall, ugly buildings. He

loses himself, finds himself then finds himself lost and has to ask a group of Polish
people under the main station the way
back to the port. He sees plaster peeling
off the old buildings in the centre like the
skin off his own sunburned lips.

Fearing the thieves he has heard about in
Naples, he keeps tight hold of the bundle
in his pocket, fingers clenched around the
notes. He has worried about looking out
of place or conspicuous and wonders
why nobody takes any notice of him. He
wonders if he has taken on a different
appearance, as if his time on the ship has
made him look like one of the natives. Not
even the Poles were surprised to see him.
He regrets not asking them if they have
any Ukrainian friends, and promises himself he will come out again and find them,
and ask them.

He doesn't want to wait too long. He is starting to feel anxious. When he was counting the captain's dollars he had heard the click of the lock opening and a throat clearing in embarrassment before seeing Sergei slip away from the door. Since then, he has moved the worn brown envelope to a new place every day. He spends a lot of time thinking about where he's going to put it next.

Once a journalist came to visit them and asked them lots of questions about life on board the ship. He brought greasy cardboard boxes with pizza in them, and bottles of beer. A few days later there was an article in the local paper, complete with a photograph showing them sitting in the deserted dining room embracing each other and grinning, but they never saw it because the journalist didn't send them a copy of the paper, even though he'd promised to.

This also meant the feverish negotiations that were going on to sell the ship and release the men also described in the article took place completely unknown to them. In oak-lined rooms with green leather chairs and air-conditioned offices with marble floors in London, Lisbon, Athens, Istanbul, Liberia and New York, faxes had tickered back and forth, talking to one another of agents and auctions, terms and conditions, get-out clauses and loopholes, prices in lira, roubles, dollars and sterling.

Sergei has often thought about trying fishing. He looks down at the narrow canal of dark water that surrounds the ship and wonders what may be swimming around in there. The froths of white and brown foam and the sickly rainbows of shiny oil that occasionally slide across the green-black surface aren't encouraging, but he's seen people fish in water much worse in Petersburg.

He rigs up a rod made from a broom handle and some twine weighed down with the broken bottom of a vodka bottle which he also hopes will act as a fly and perches on the edge of the *Neva Star* and sits there for hours, fishing without catching anything. Once, he sees an enormous grey cod, evidently lost, but it doesn't bite. Every now and then he pulls up the twine to check. There's nothing to use as bait. He thinks that might be why he doesn't catch anything.

He wonders what any fish who might live in the waters of the port of Naples would eat and what he would find in the belly of a fish he caught when he gutted it with his penknife. Bones, little fish, jewels.

As he sits there fishing he thinks about the money he saw Sergei counting and wonders where it came from and where he's hidden it now. He sees a girl sitting on the deck of yacht passing in the distance and she reminds him of the mermaid he saw sitting on a rock in Copenhagen. She reminds him of Masha, and he wonders what his wife is doing now. He wonders why she left him after his friend Sergei had been to visit, and why he never told Sergei she'd left.

After the article in the newspaper, the sailors became a minor tourist attraction. Small groups of people came to look at them and waved to them from the shore.

They would wave back, and the two groups would shout things to each other in mutually incomprehensible languages. After a while, though, the novelty faded and people stopped dropping by. Now they've become such a fixture that people don't even see them there any more. In the future, people will tell stories of the three Russian sailors who spent three years on a boat in the port of Naples.

Sergei thinks that if anybody should ask him where he lives now, he would still say in that house in Odessa. That's where I live, he'd say, there in that house with its high windows and wooden floor and the old stove we light in the winter to keep warm. That's where I live, with my mother and my little sister. He would get out the picture he keeps with him and show the house with its moulded ceilings and crumbling arches and the dark entrance hall where the old *dežurnaja* who never speaks lives. Nobody asks him where he lives.

Sergei knows that this is siren land, that he is stranded in a city founded when the mermaid Parthenope fell in love with one of Odysseus' men who ignored her by blocking his ears and sailing right past her. She was so heartbroken she cried until she died and her body was washed up on a rock here.

Rust wears the bow, salt eats up the paint on the hull. There are no seagulls to make any sound, as there is nothing to scavenge. The only sounds you can hear on the *Neva Star* are the distant roar of traffic from the city, the creak of fatiguing metal, the sea sweating oil in summer, the gnaw of advancing decay.

Sergei slinks out after dark and heads back to the station where he met the Poles. At night, there is no one there but a few drunks. He tries asking them if they know any Ukrainians round here, but nobody answers him apart from a man with a face so red and swollen Sergei fears he is about to explode. He recognises Sergei's accent, tells him he is from Moldova and they start speaking in Russian. Sergei says he's been stuck on a boat in the port for three years. The man with the red face tells him a story that he's heard in Naples. Once there was a boy called Cola Pesce. Cola Pesce loved diving down and swimming for hours and hours in the waters of the bay of Naples. His mother got fed up with him doing nothing but sploshing around in the water all day and said that if he didn't give up he'd turn into a fish. That's why they called him Cola Pesce. Cola dived deep down into the water and let a huge fish swallow him up. Then he travelled all over the world, under the sea, in the belly of the fish before eventually getting out his knife and cutting himself free. When the king heard about Cola Pesce's talent he demanded to see him. 'Tell me,' he asked the boy, 'what does the bottom of the sea look like?', and Cola Pesce replied that it was filled with gardens of coral, wrecks of ships, pieces of amber, phosphorescent fish and precious stones scattered about among the bones of drowned sailors. The king told him to go down again and bring up some of the treasure for him, but Cola immediately had a bad feeling. 'If I go down again,' he told the king, 'I'll never come back up', but the king insisted and Cola went down again. In some versions of the story he takes down a handful of lentils with him, in others a piece of wood, in others a drop of blood, and he says that if this thing rises to the surface before I do, then I shall be dead. The lentils, the piece of wood, the drop of blood float to the surface. They're still waiting for him to come back up.

Sergei gave the red-faced man some of his money, and headed quickly back for the ship, making sure he didn't get lost on the way.

Shipwrecked on board a ship, stranded afloat under a flag of inconvenience, they listen out for visitors bringing them good news. They hear only unquiet ghosts, snoring sailors. The fax machines, once chattering about the sailors' fate, have stopped their ticking now, ink fading on sheets of curling white paper piled up on dusty office floors or chewed up by the long sharp teeth of shredding machines. No emails pass back and forth, no agents or intermediaries discuss the case.

Every day Sergei walks out onto the deck of the *Neva Star* and looks out across the bay. He fills himself up with the luminous intensity of the big silver mornings, watching the rigs and funnels of other ships, the hunched cranes and walls of containers on the docks, the wide flat mirror of water in the port basin and the broken-topped triangle of Mount Vesuvius in the distance. He thinks it's one of the most beautiful things he's ever seen, and thinks about how it would be to live here forever and spend every morning looking out at that looming shadow. He thinks about the money that has been stashed away and gets moved every day and where it came from and what will happen to it. He wonders how many Poles and Ukrainians and Romanians and Russians and Turks and Cubans and Albanians and Portuguese and people from everywhere and nowhere there are in the city, how they got there and what they do there. He wonders how many other sailors are stuck on other ships in other ports in other parts of the world and how they got there and what they do there. He ponders over what may or may not have happened to the captain. He remembers his brief wife Tatiana, Masha's face after he'd kissed her and

Sorin's friend's Venetian wife. He thinks about legends of mermaids and mermen, at home neither in the sea nor on the land. He thinks that being on board a ship is like leaving and leaving and leaving and never arriving anywhere.

C. D. ROSE was born in Manchester at the tail end of the 1960s. Since then, he has lived and worked in half a dozen different countries. He has published stories with Galley Beggar and Comma Press, and he edited *The Biographical Dictionary of Literary Failure*, published by Melville House. He is at home anywhere there are dark bars, dusty second-hand bookshops, and a good library.

DAUNT BOOKS

Founded in 2010, the Daunt Books imprint
is dedicated to discovering brilliant works by
talented authors from around the world.
Whether reissuing beautiful new editions of
lost classics or introducing fresh literary
voices, we're drawn to writing that evokes a
strong sense of place – novels, short fiction,
memoirs, travel accounts, and translations
with a lingering atmosphere, a thrilling
story, and a distinctive style. With our roots
as a travel bookshop, the titles we publish
are inspired by the Daunt shops themselves,
and the exciting atmosphere of discovery
to be found in a good bookshop.

For more information, please visit
www.dauntbookspublishing.co.uk

ALSO PUBLISHED BY
DAUNT BOOKS

Saki *Improper Stories*
Sybille Bedford *A Favourite of the Gods*
Jií Weil *Mendelssohn is on the Roof*
Sybille Bedford *A Compass Error*
Mark Twain *American Drolleries*
C. S. Godshalk *Kalimantaan*
Jií Weil *Life With A Star*
Ann Bridge *Illyrian Spring*
Paul Watkins *Calm at Sunset, Calm at Dawn*
Stefan Heym *The Architects*
O. Henry *A Dance of Folly and Pleasure*
K J Orr *The Inland Sea*
Christa Wolf *Cassandra*
Simon Loftus *The Invention of Memory*
G. B. Stern *The Matriarch*
Virginia Woolf *The London Scene*
Philip Langeskov *Barcelona*
Nathanael West *Miss Lonelyhearts*

Mahesh Rao *The Smoke is Rising*
James Buchan *A Good Place to Die*
Sybille Bedford *Pleasures and Landscapes*
Sarah Pickstone *Park Notes*
Madeleine Bourdouxhe *La Femme de Gilles*
S. N. Behrman *Duveen*
Julianne Pachico *The Tourists*
Machado de Assis *Dom Casmurro*
Laura van den Berg *The Isle of Youth*
Bapsi Sidhwa *The Crow Eaters*
Ann Bridge *Peking Picnic*
Leonard Michaels *Sylvia*
John McPhee *Coming into the Country*
Vivian Gornick *Fierce Attachments*
Mahesh Rao *One Point Two Billion*
John Collier *His Monkey Wife*